Señor Pancho Had a Rancho

by René Colato Laínez

illustrated by Elwood Smith

Holiday House / New York

*To all Panchos and Panchitos—especially Francisco Erik—
who like to sing, play, and explore. —R. C. L.*

For Maggie, who helps me till the soil.—E. S.

Printed and Bound in April 2013 at Tien Wah Press, Johor Bahru, Johor, Malaysia.
The text typeface is Orenga.
The artwork was created with waterproof India ink on Arches 90# cold press watercolor paper using a Pelikan 250 fountain pen with a medium or fine nib and Pelikan transparent pan watercolors applied with a Kolinsky sable watercolor brush. The final art was scanned into Photoshop and merged with separate layers of watercolor textures and backgrounds created by the artist.
www.holidayhouse.com
First Edition
1 3 5 7 9 10 8 6 4 2

Library of Congress Cataloging-in-Publication Data
Colato Laínez, René.
Señor Pancho had a rancho / by René Colato Laínez ; illustrated by Elwood Smith. — 1st ed.
p. cm.
Summary: As Old MacDonald sings of farm animals that moo and woof, Señor Pancho sings of those that jii and guau, until the animals realize they understand each other and get together for a fiesta.
ISBN 978-0-8234-2632-4 (hardcover)
[1. Stories in rhyme. 2. Domestic animals—Fiction. 3. Animal sounds—Fiction.
4. Bilingualism—Fiction.] I. Smith, Elwood H., 1941- ill. II. Title.
PZ8.3.C668Sen 2013
 [E]—dc23
2012007672

Glossary

farm – rancho or granja
(RAHN-cho) (GRAHN-hah)

hello – hola (OH-lah)

a – un, una (OON, OON-ah)

rooster – gallo (GAH-yoh)

dog – perro (PEHRR-oh)

sheep – oveja (oh-VEH-hah)

horse – caballo (cah-BAH-yoh)

chick – pollito (poh-YEE-toh)

cow – vaca (VAH-kah)

let's dance – vamos a bailar
(VAH-mohs ah beye-LAHR)

Pronunciation guide for Spanish sounds

quiquiriquí – *kee-kee-ree-KEE*

guau guau – *wow wow*

bee bee – *beh-eh beh-eh*

jii jii – *hee-ee hee-ee*

pío pío – *pEE-oh pEE-oh*

muu muu – *moo moo*

Old MacDonald had a farm, E-I-E-I-O.
Hello!

Señor Pancho had a *rancho*, cha-cha-cha-cha-cha.
¡Hola!

Old MacDonald had a farm, E-I-E-I-O.
And on his farm he had a rooster, E-I-E-I-O.
With a cock-a-doodle-doo here and a cock-a-doodle-doo there.
Here a cock-a-doodle-doo, there a cock-a-doodle-doo.
Everywhere a cock-a-doodle-doo.

Señor Pancho had a *rancho, cha-cha-cha-cha-cha.*
And on his *rancho* he had *un gallo, cha-cha-cha-cha-cha.*
With a *quiquiriquí* here and a *quiquiriquí* there.
Here a *quiquiriquí,* there a *quiquiriquí.*
Everywhere a *quiquiriquí.*

Old MacDonald had a farm, E-I-E-I-O.
And on his farm he had a dog, E-I-E-I-O.
With a woof, woof here and a woof, woof there.
Here a woof, there a woof.
Everywhere a woof, woof.

Señor Pancho had a *rancho*, *cha-cha-cha-cha-cha*.
And on his *rancho* he had *un perro*, *cha-cha-cha-cha-cha*.
With a *guau guau* here and a *guau guau* there.
Here a *guau*, there a *guau*.
Everywhere a *guau guau*.

Old MacDonald had a farm, E-I-E-I-O.
And on his farm he had a sheep, E-I-E-I-O.
With a baa, baa here and a baa, baa there.
Here a baa, there a baa.
Everywhere a baa, baa.

Señor Pancho had a *rancho*, *cha-cha-cha-cha-cha.*
And on his *rancho* he had *una oveja*, *cha-cha-cha-cha-cha.*
With a *bee bee* here and a *bee bee* there.
Here a *bee*, there a *bee*.
Everywhere a *bee bee*.

Old MacDonald had a farm, E-I-E-I-O.
And on his farm he had a horse, E-I-E-I-O.
With a neigh, neigh here and a neigh, neigh there.
Here a neigh, there a neigh.
Everywhere a neigh, neigh.

Señor Pancho had a *rancho*, *cha-cha-cha-cha-cha*.
And on his *rancho* he had *un caballo*, *cha-cha-cha-cha-cha*.
With a *jii jii* here and a *jii jii* there.
Here a *jii*, there a *jii*.
Everywhere a *jii jii*.

Old MacDonald had a farm, E-I-E-I-O.
And on his farm he had a chick, E-I-E-I-O.
With a peep, peep here and a peep, peep there.
Here a peep, there a peep.
Everywhere a peep, peep.

Señor Pancho had a *rancho*, *cha-cha-cha-cha-cha*.
And on his *rancho* he had *un pollito*, *cha-cha-cha-cha-cha*.
With a *pío pío* here and a *pío pío* there.
Here a *pío*, there a *pío*.
Everywhere a *pío pío*.

Old MacDonald had a farm, E-I-E-I-O.
And on his farm he had a cow, E-I-E-I-O.
With a moo, moo here and a moo, moo there.
Here a moo, there a moo.
Everywhere a moo, moo.

Señor Pancho had a *rancho*, cha-cha-cha-cha-cha.
And on his *rancho* he had *una vaca*, cha-cha-cha-cha-cha.
With a *muu muu* here and a *muu muu* there.
Here a *muu*, there a *muu*.
Everywhere a *muu muu*.
Moo, moo? ¿*Muu muu*?

Old MacDonald had a farm, E-I-E-I-O.
Señor Pancho had a *rancho*, *cha-cha-cha-cha-cha*.
And on their farms they had a cow and *una vaca* too.
With a moo, moo here and a *muu muu* there.
Here a moo, there a *muu*.
Everywhere a moo *muu*.

Old MacDonald had a farm, E-I-E-I-O.
Señor Pancho had a *rancho, cha-cha-cha-cha-cha.*
With a moo, moo here and a *muu muu* there.
With a cock-a-doodle-doo here and a *quiquiriquí* there.

With a woof, woof here and a *guau guau* there.
With a baa, baa here and a *bee bee* there.
With a neigh, neigh here and a *jii jii* there.
With a peep, peep here and a *pío pío* there.

"*¡Vamos a bailar!*"

"Let's dance!"

Author's Note

"Old MacDonald Had a Farm" has been a favorite children's song for more than three hundred years.

The song is popular around the world and is sung by children in many languages. In each different language, animals have their own unique sounds—this version was inspired by my own bilingual students, who speak both English and Spanish!

This book is a celebration of languages. In every celebration, we need music and dance. Even though I-A-I-A-O is the most popular translation in Spanish for E-I-E-I-O, I wanted Señor Pancho to have his unique phrase. I had several options and it was hard to choose one. I asked my students, and they voted for *cha-cha-cha-cha-cha* while they danced around the classroom. Now the celebration was complete. Will you join Señor Pancho and Old MacDonald? *Cha-cha-cha-cha-cha!*

saludos,

René Colato Laínez